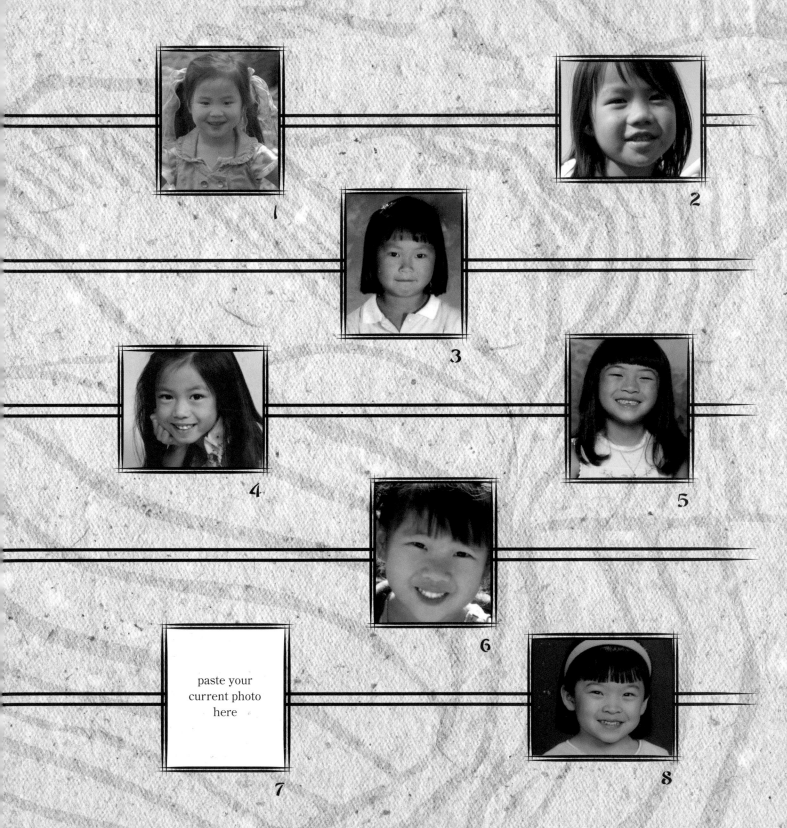

This book is dedicated to my granddaughter Vi-yen

Lydia
Kate
Isabel
Marie
Anna
Maggy
Lucie
Abby
Nicole
Annalise
Halle
Maggie
Addair
Kaili

and my other grandchildren.

Acknowledgements

Kristin Blackwood • Mike Blanc • Trio Design & Marketing Communications, Inc., Jennie Levy Smith
Dave Shoenfelt • Dr. Ivonne Hobfoll, Clinical Psychologist, Summa Health System • Dr. Janet Stadulis
Paul Royer • Kurt Landefeld • Sheila Tarr • Michael Olin-Hitt • Larry Chilnick
Strauss Consultants, Karen Strauss • Holt International

Made In China

A Story of Adoption

by

Vanita Oelschlager

illustrated by

Kristin Blackwood

VanitaBooks, LLC

My big sister played
with me in my room.

We played clean up the house
with my sweeper and broom.

On the broom there were words.
I asked what they said.

"Made in China" is what
my big sister read.

I saw the same words
on most of my things:
my teacups, my play food,
my dolly that sings.

"It's just like you,"
    my big sister said,
"You're Made in China.
    It's stamped right on your head."

She teased me some more.
"You're like my shirt
and favorite plaid skirt."

She showed me the tags,
and that really hurt.

I'll go see my dad
and ask if it's so.

I went to my dad,
and I asked him straight out,
"Was I 'Made in China'?
What's she talking about?"

He said, "Well, I can see
how you'd think that is true.
But you're much more than what
people say about you."

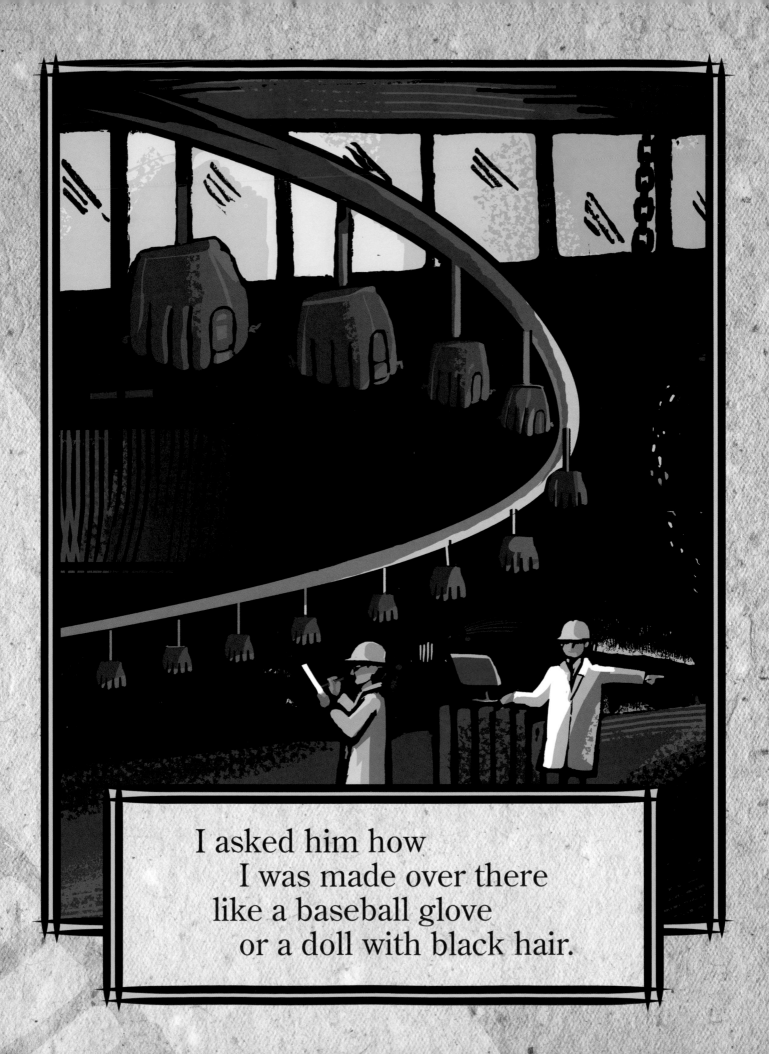

I asked him how
        I was made over there
like a baseball glove
        or a doll with black hair.

He said, "Sweetheart,
      you're not made like a toy.
You were 'Made in China'
      to bring us joy.

You were born in China
in a town called Ningdu
to a wonderful woman
who really loved you.

In China she couldn't take care of you, so she did a hard thing when she let you go.

And way over here
we waited, you see,
for you to become
part of our family.

Your mother in China
gave you your smile.

Now you're with us forever,
not just for a while.

So, yes, my love,
   I guess that it's true.
You were 'Made in China'
   but not like a shoe.

Not of plastic or cloth
but from a love so deep
it will never be lost,
when you're awake or asleep.

Please, my dear one,
don't ever be sad.
You were 'Made in China'
so I'd be your dad.

And if ever you feel
	you are not loved here,
you just come to me,
	and I'll make it clear-

We love you now,
    we loved you before.
In all the wide world
    we couldn't love you more."

Author Vanita Oelschlager and illustrator Kristin Blackwood are mother and daughter, and have collaborated on many children's books. This book reflects their sensitivity to adopted children. Kristin's second daughter is adopted from China.

To learn about conflict resolution, please look on our website:VanitaBooks.com.

About the author

Vanita Oelschlager is a wife, mother, grandmother, businesswoman, former teacher, current caregiver, author, and poet. She is a graduate of Mt. Union College in Alliance, Ohio, where she currently serves as a Trustee. Her latest book, *My Grampy Can't Walk*, is an uplifting story about the unique relationship between her husband, Jim, who has multiple sclerosis, and their grandchildren. Vanita is also Writer in Residence for Literacy Programs at the University of Akron.

About the illustrator

Kristin Blackwood is an experienced illustrator whose other books include: *My Grampy Can't Walk*, *Let Me Bee*, and *What Pet Will I Get?*. She has a degree from Kent State University in Art History. In addition to teaching and her design work, Kristin enjoys being a mother to her two daughters.

Kristin's illustration is a blending of techniques, beginning with traditional block prints, cut in linoleum, and printed in black on white stock. The images were converted to digital format through flatbed scanning. Color layering was added using Corel® Painter™, and Adobe® Photoshop®, computer software for digital illustration. Background supports were created by overlaying the block print images on photographed pineapple paper from the iStockphoto® archive. The result, presented here, strikes a rich visual note for *Made In China*.

About Holt International

In addition to being one of the leading international adoption agencies, Holt International also develops and maintains programs overseas to give orphaned, abandoned and vulnerable children safe and nurturing environments in which to develop. Each year, Holt helps more that 3,000 children in China through its foster care programs; HIV/AIDS-support programs; urgent medical care for malnourished babies and children in orphanages; surgeries to correct clubfoot, and cleft lips and palates; treatment of congenital heart conditions; family preservation; intercountry adoption and in many other ways.

All profits from this book will benefit Holt International's work in China.

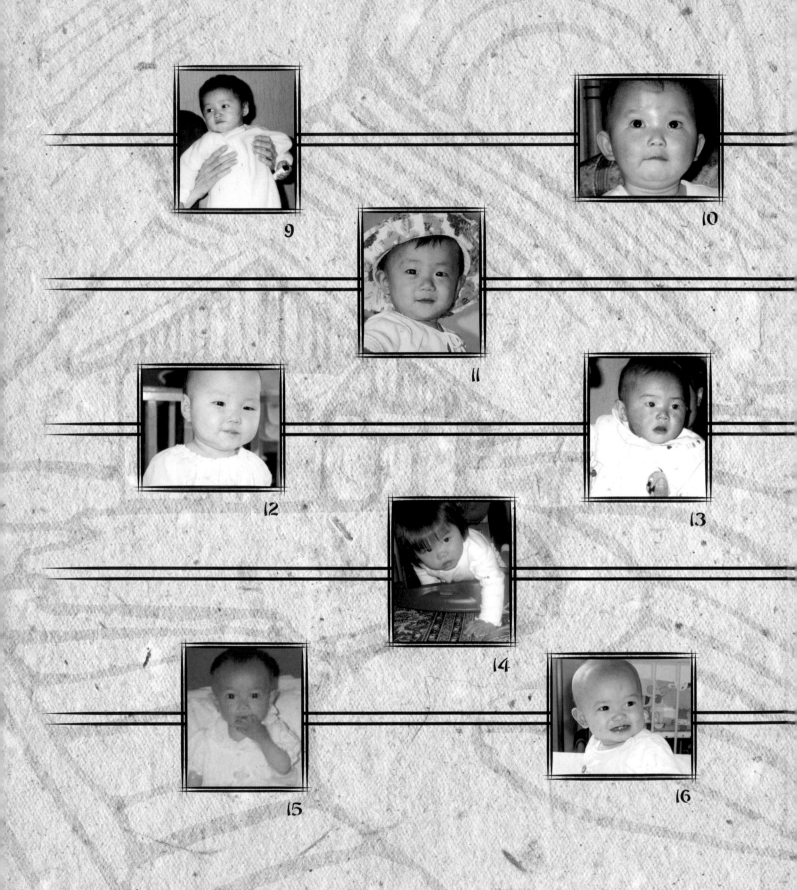